FREEDOM TRAIL

For my mother
and for
Margaret Van Duyne

*The general situation and most of the events described in
this book are drawn directly from historical facts. However,
the fictional characters are wholly imaginative: they do not
portray and are not intended to portray any actual persons.*

© 1958 by Nancy Coy
All rights reserved

No part of this book may be reproduced in any form
without permission in writing from the publisher

Library of Congress Catalog Card Number: 57-5414

Printed in the United States of America
by The Cornwall Press, Inc., Cornwall, N. Y.

1

☆

WHERE THE ROAD ran north to danger, John Trimble flattened himself against a tree. Brown gloom tunneled the road under the pines and smudged the wiry figure in buckskin. Before him towered the safe bulk of French Mountain, but as he studied the steep western bluffs, he frowned. Across the mountain barrier, up the lakes, was the enemy, waiting.

French Mountain blocked the morning sun and shadowed the woods along its foot. The shadow was strong. It sheltered the track to the Trimbles' mill and stretched toward the mill itself, hidden on the other side of the valley. The mill made gunpowder, and gunpowder was scarce in the American army. Every grain was needed.

Cradling his bundle, John watched. Once across the military road, he was safe, but no one, friend or enemy, must see him reach the secret track. Was that someone now? Hastily, he tossed the bundle toward a cedar thicket, crawled after it and let the branches go, scuffing his buckskin shirt as he worked his way in.

Between the branches, he could watch both the hidden entrance to the mill track and the road that led around French Mountain to Lake George, then on through miles of wilderness to Lake Champlain and Canada. In Canada was their leader and he meant to split the colonies in two.

"British are on the Lake now," John added, "waiting for Indians to join them."

"Then it's true, the British have turned the Indians loose on us. Just because we've got the spunk to stand up for our rights. Heathen devils!" Ike fairly spat out, rubbing his leg. "We'll fix em. They lamed my leg in the old French wars. And there's many like me. We've a score to settle with them."

He struck John on the shoulder. "Don't you fret, lad. The British may have Indians, but we have Ti. They won't get by Ti—not with us making powder for the cannon. Nothing frightens the Indians more than those big guns."

John grinned. "Boom, and they'll run away."

"Right!" Ike nodded. "But your mother now, how does she take this?"

"Last night Mother cried *Indians* and grabbed up the baby. But I can shoot straight, so she ought not to be afraid, even with Father away. Father went to Fort George to get guards for the mill."

"It's natural for your mother to be frightened. Didn't she tell you about hiding in the fireplace oven when she was a little girl? Indians right in the house, whooping and smashing things up with their tomahawks. If she hadn't been smart enough to hide in the oven, they would have caught her."

"It must have been exciting, though." John sighed. "I wish I could join the army and fight Indians."

"Huh, excitement. You'll get plenty before the war's done. You want to see the mill working?"

John nodded eagerly. "You mean I can? Father said to stay away unless you tell me it's safe."

4

Ike led the way to the mill door. "Nothing to explode now. I'm just stamping saltpeter, taking out the lumps so it will mix better with charcoal and sulphur."

"Father says you could make more powder if you had more sulphur."

"True." Ike shook his head sadly, "but we're lucky to have enough saltpeter. If that man down the valley hadn't found an easy way to make it, we'd be in trouble. The British would have us back under their thumb quick. Now we can get fourteen pounds of saltpeter from three bushels of dirt."

"Any dirt? Like this?" John scuffed up a shower of it.

Ike laughed. "Of course not, silly, dirt from barns and chicken houses. Come along now."

They went into the gloomy mill, where a shaft from the water wheel turned big wooden stampers that were pounding saltpeter into fine grains. The stampers went *thump, thump, thump* until John's ears sang with the noise. How could Ike stand it all day?

"We do the same when we mix the powder," yelled Ike. "That's when it's dangerous, but we're careful when we wet it down. Nothing's exploded yet."

"Ike, listen. I saw Indians on the trail." John described the runners.

Ike questioned him sharply and frowned. "Going north fast. Most likely, messengers to Burgoyne from the Iroquois. What else would they be, going north? It sounds bad. General Schuyler's been trying to keep the Indians friendly, but—"

Ike stopped to shut the door. "It takes presents, and Congress has no money for presents. The British give out clothes and powder and rum. Indians say you must make your promise solid with gifts, if you mean to keep it.

One friendly with the British probably, most of them were. What crazy thing had he started, bringing an Indian home to his own family, perhaps an enemy to his own house? Maybe the Indian did not even come from the west. Maybe he came from the British Army, across the slope of French Mountain. He might have turned around as he fell.

John took Ashara's hand and put it again around his own shoulder. "Friend," he said, "come."

Ashara nodded. Slowly, painfully, he staggered with his guide to the Trimble cabin.

2

☆

GLIMPSED THROUGH THE TREES, the cabin was a welcome sight, with its weather-beaten logs and cedar shingles holding snug to the ground. Struggling under Ashara's weight, John climbed the fence that surrounded the cleared ground and dragged the Indian after him.

In the dooryard, John's mother stood shaking a basket of cornmeal. "Here, chick—here, chick," she called as a row of puffballs fluttered around her. Then, catching sight of Ashara, she cried out, "No!" and dropped the basket. With a yellow flurry of wings, the chickens scatterd.

8

"John, what do you mean by bringing an Indian here? You know I won't have it."

Ashara stiffened. "I go." But as he dropped his hold on John, his legs buckled under him and, with a startled look, he slid to the ground.

"Good heavens!" exclaimed Mistress Trimble, ignoring the chickens, who now crowded greedily around the basket. "What have I said? He's only a boy, if he is an Indian. I don't believe he's a day older than you."

"I'm not so young," muttered John under his breath.

"He looks starved. Take his shoulders, and I'll carry his legs. Mary," she called to the little girl peeping from behind the door, "pull out the trundle bed."

Mistress Trimble shuddered as she touched the Indian, but lifting his legs, she hurried through the kitchen, with Ashara's body dangling between her and John. Mary ran ahead, to drag the trundle bed from under the big one and hold it steady while they laid the Indian down. Still limp, he did not move.

Mistress Trimble looked down at the blood-smeared face. "Where did you find him?" Her voice was sharp.

"On the hill slope, across the valley from French Mountain, near the mill."

"French Mountain, did he come over it?" she murmured. Then, tucking the covers in, she felt the Indian's forehead. "He has some fever. Should I give him Feverfew? No, I'll try plain mush. You stay here, John, while I get it."

When she returned with a bowl of cornmeal mush and a wooden spoon, the Indian looked at her impassively. She held out a spoonful of mush. Ashara pressed his mouth tight shut, until Mistress Trimble put down the spoon.

"I'm sorry I spoke as I did," she said hesitantly. "John says you can talk English, so you probably understand a

9

good deal more. We want to help you get well. Please eat the mush."

"*Orrichwio*—good," said Ashara. He smiled and opened his lips. As fast as the spoon could travel from bowl to mouth, he swallowed the mush. "John friend. Mother good. *Niawo*—I say thanks."

When the bowl was emptied and Ashara asleep, Mistress Trimble beckoned John from the room. She paused in the kitchen, then shook her head.

"The Indian may only feign sleep," she whispered and led John outside. Once in the yard, she turned with a whirl of blue skirts.

"Son, I do not know what to say. How can you bring him here, right to our house, when the powder mill is so close and so important? Your father will be furious."

"Father?" gasped John. "He's coming home?"

"I sent Ned after him. He will not like leaving his work. The Indian may be only a sick boy, but probably he's a spy."

"A spy," John shouted. "Oh, no!"

"*Ssh*," his mother whispered. "Say nothing to anyone until your father comes."

"No, no," John stammered. "He's not. I know he's not. He was hurt when I found him. What else could I do? You'd not want me to leave him there hurt?"

Rubbing dirt circles with his toe, John looked sideways at his mother. He wanted to say, "You take care of everything that's sick, even that starved kitten Mary found. People come to you for herbs and pills and care. I know you wouldn't want me to leave Ashara," but the words would not come out. He rubbed another dirt circle. His mother waited quietly, a little smile on her face.

"I—I did think of Ike," John spoke at last. "But then

Ashara would be right at the mill. He'd learn about it. Just the same, he's not a spy."

"Ashara, is that his name? I suppose you had to bring him," Mistress Trimble agreed. But why did the Indian have to be found? He meant danger to them all. As if the British to the north were not threat enough, they had a spy in their house.

"Ashara means knife," John went on.

"Knife? God send it be not a knife pointed at our fort!" Mistress Trimble hugged John to her, quickly, for she knew that he felt he was too big to be babied. "I hope you're right, Son—for all our sakes, but mostly for yours."

"Did you hear that?" John turned quickly. The faint hoofbeats sounded like his father's mare, Black Bet.

"It must be the captain. Tell him everything, just as it happened. I'll go back and watch the Indian." Mistress Trimble hurried off.

John's heart felt queer, as though it had gone somewhere down near his feet, he guessed. He peered along the trail, almost lost between the trees. Hoofbeats drummed as Captain Trimble burst into the clearing. At the sight of his son, he pulled up short. He was so angry that his words fairly tumbled out. "What kind of tomfool prank is this? Bringing an Indian to our very house. You know how your mother feels about Indians. Why do you frighten her? He's a spy. No other reason for him to be here."

John tipped back his head to look up at his tall father on the tall horse. "I didn't mean to frighten Mother. I brought Ashara because he needs help, and she can cure anything. I—I didn't stop to think," he ended miserably.

"That's just it. You do things first and think afterwards. I thought you were improving, but this is impossible. What

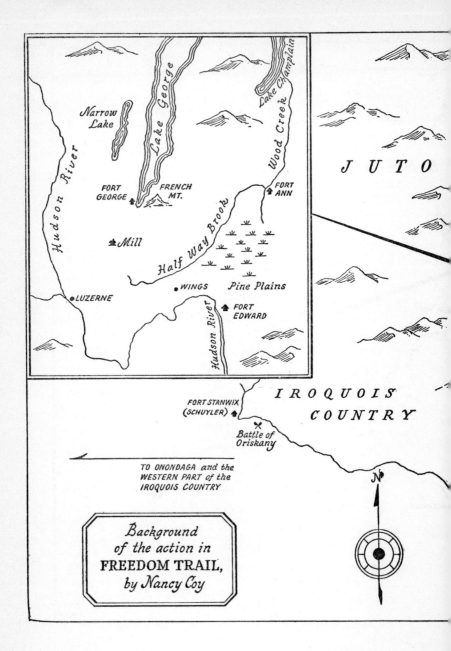

Background
of the action in
FREEDOM TRAIL,
by Nancy Coy

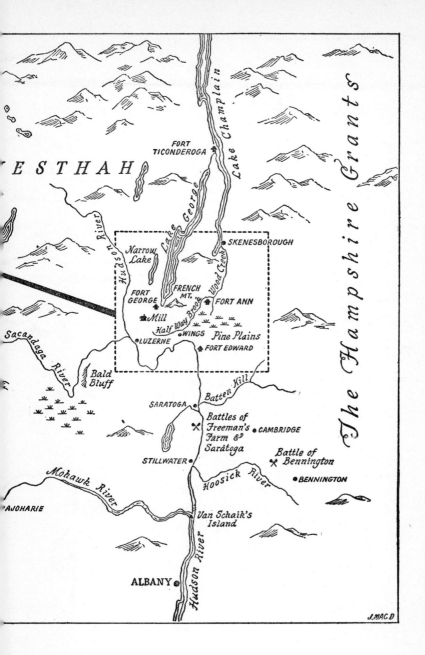

are we to do with your spy? Send him to Burgoyne's army?"

"I—" John hung his head. No, indecision would never do, just because his father was angry. He clenched his fists and plucked up courage.

"He's not a spy, Father. I'm sure of that. I found him hurt. But I did see two Indian runners, heading for the Lake."

Captain Trimble sighed. "I'm sorry, Son, anger won't help. Now that he's here, we must put up with it. You had better tell me the whole story, then I'll take a look at your Indian." (Unless the rogue has decamped, he muttered to himself.) He climbed wearily down from Black Bet and, handing his son the reins, started toward the house. John noticed that the mare's coat was dirty and her mane and tail were tangled. The soldiers had little time for grooming.

Pushing her head against John, Bet whuffled hopefully. "Nothing for you right now, girl," he whispered. He held tightly to the horse as he walked beside his father and told of his seeing the two Indians on the move and finding Ashara.

Captain Trimble listened with no change of expression. He put in a question or two, but he gave John no sign of his thoughts until the story was done.

"Well, perhaps you couldn't help bringing him here," the captain said finally. "I still feel doubtful about him, but at least he's under our eyes. You must watch him, John, but try not to make him suspicious. Keep him from slipping off. I must go back to Albany or I would not leave the task to you."

"But, Father, I ought to fight. Can't I go join the army?

Jim Park went yesterday, and Donald Macomber; they're the same age as I am."

"You want to go with Jim Park?" Captain Trimble was startled. "Didn't they tell you where? No, I can see not." The captain looked sadly at his son, as if he wanted to tell him something, but did not know how to word it. "You like them, don't you?"

"Oh, yes." John nodded emphatically. "Can't I join? Ned can do what I do."

Captain Trimble shook his head. "You can't go now and leave Mother alone with the Indian. You didn't think when you said that. I agree that Ned can run the errands, but he can't shoot so well. Ask the Indian—Ashara, did you call him? That sounds like an Onondaga name—ask Ashara to teach you his language. Now, Son, let me look at him and get something to eat. Take care of Black Bet."

John dropped the reins over a fence post and ran for the curry comb. By the time he was finished, the mare would glow like satin, but he was still hard at work when he heard his father.

"Bet, aren't you glad we came home?" As Black Bet stamped her foot, John looked up, all his face a question.

"The Indian was asleep. No marks on him, so I couldn't tell anything about his tribe. John, read this, but don't let your mother see it. Burgoyne's at Bouquet River. He put out this piece of boastfulness." Captain Trimble pulled from his waistcoat pocket a crumpled piece of paper and, with a glance toward the house, pushed it into his son's hand. Leaning against Black Bet, so that she shielded him from view, John unfolded it with eager fingers. He muttered rapidly, "By John Burgoyne, Esquire, Lieutenant General of his Majesty's armys . . . the forces entrusted to my command . . . present unnatural rebellion . . ."

15

Then his voice rose angrily. "Listen to this: 'I have but to give stretch to the Indian forces under my direction and they amount to thousands, to overtake the hardened enemies of Great Britain, wherever they may lurk. . . . The messengers of justice and wrath await them.'" John slammed the paper together and shoved it toward his father.

"Burgoyne turns the Indians loose on us and then boasts of it!" he stormed. "But they can't get past Ti, can they? Bouquet River, where is that?"

"North of Ti," Captain Trimble answered as he pulled the reins off the fence post. "The army can't get past, but his Indians will sift through the woods around the fort. That's why you must watch this one. He looks honest, but keep an eye on him."

John watched his father out of the clearing. Not to join the American Army, when the enemy was near! Then his thoughts brightened. Ashara could not be a spy. Even his father, who called him one, said the Indian boy looked honest. Perhaps he and Ashara could be true friends. Did that word mean friend that Ashara used?

John tried it. *"Ungiatshi."* But how could he explain that he wanted to be friends? That he trusted the Indian and was risking his family's safety because of that trust? After all, Ashara had as much reason to be suspicious of them as they had of him. It was so hard to talk, how could he show the Indian? John snapped his fingers and laughed. He knew how. He pulled it out, his hunting knife, sharp enough to cut bone, shining clean, not a speck of rust. But could he bear to part with it?

John rubbed the blade. That was the gift for Ashara, a new knife for a broken one, a steel knife for a flint one. Clutching it, he fairly ran into the house.

"Ashara still asleep?" he asked his mother.

"Yes, but it's time for him to eat. You go wake him. I made him some succotash."

From the edge of the trundle bed, John studied the sleeping boy. He had no idea how Indian faces should look, but this one seemed open and straight-forward. Ashara was no spy. John would stake his life on that.

The Indian stirred. "John," he murmured. "*Ungiatshi.*"

"Friend," John said in English. "I brought you a present. You broke yours, so maybe you will like this one."

Ashara said nothing. He just stared at the white boy, paying no attention to what he held.

John's heart sank. He had chosen the wrong gift, spoiled things. "It has a good edge," he asserted, rubbing the handle. "It cuts fine."

Then Ashara looked down. "Knife," he muttered, "*Wasto* knife." He pushed his clenched fist against his chest. "Give Ashara?"

John smiled. "Give Ashara. A knife for The Knife."

Ashara laughed. Then he frowned and spoke rapidly in his own language. The words sounded sharp and angry. Surprised at his own boldness, John asked what he meant. Ashara said, "Knife broken. You make knife whole. Now I think this. New knife. I go back, show tribe, prove tribe wrong."

Wrong about what? But John dared not ask.

"This your one knife? No more," Ashara guessed shrewdly.

John dodged the question. "I want you to have it. That's all right."

"You my friend," Ashara went on. "*Jatattege*—brother." For the first time, he touched the knife and, with his other hand, suddenly seized the white boy's wrist. John felt fire flash across the vein.

"Oh!" he gasped and watched blood ooze slowly out. Ashara cut his own wrist, dropped the knife and held the two streams together.

"Brother," he said again, but he shook a disapproving head. "Warrior not say 'oh.' Enemy hear, enemy laugh if warrior say 'oh.' When we go on warpath together, be silent."

John sat in dazed surprise. "I didn't know what you were going to do," he explained. "You want me to be your brother?"

"Brother save my life," said Ashara simply. "Now I give brother new name. Indian name, easy to say. Brother has red hair. Onondaga word for red hair—*Otquechtarocu onuchquirote*." His eyes glinted with mischief. "Hair hot, temper hot. *Otquechtarocu onuchquirote* too long, so I say *Otquechtarocu*. Word short, means red."

"Oquetocu." John tried to say it, but his head spun. A blood brother and a new name, all at once.

"*Otquechtarocu*," Ashara corrected sternly. "You know how to throw tomahawk?"

"No."

"I teach. We—" The joy faded from his face. "Ashara no tomahawk."

"I can get one from Ike. Ike's nice. He's over at—" John stopped and bit his tongue. He had almost given the secret away.

Ashara waited, then grinned. "Warrior keep still tongue. Good."

"Ashara, where are you from? Have you been to war?" John burst out.

Ashara looked blank. "Some day I tell you. Now you get tomahawk. Tomorrow I teach. Now I sleep." He lay down and turned his face away.

With a heavy heart, the white boy tiptoed across the pine floor. Had he been too impulsive again, too curious? But Ashara had promised to teach him how to throw a tomahawk. The first thing in the morning, he would go borrow Ike's.

3

☆

SO THAT'S WHY you want Ike—to borrow his tomahawk."

"Yes, that's why, and what right have you got to stop me, Ben Wills?" John doubled his fists. Ben had better move away from that mill door.

The two faced each other, with the shadow of the water wheel falling across them. Ben topped John by a head. He was enough taller to let the light shine full on his sulky face and narrow eyes, while John was all in shadow, except for one sunbeam turning his red top to fire.

"Every right. You want to give it to your Indian friend so he can knock us all on the head." Ben spread his feet firm before the door. He had no idea of letting John squeeze past. John glared back. He could hear, inside the mill, the steady thump of the stampers. Ike must be there, and Ike said he could borrow the tomahawk any time he wanted to.

"He's a spy," Ben yelled. "He's a spy and you're an Injun lover. You don't care if we all get killed."

"I'm giving him a fair chance, but not you. You call spy before you know."

"Injun lover!" Forgetting to guard the door, Ben danced up and down. "Injun lover! Injun lover!"

John saw red. Take an insult like that, even if Ben was huskier and often beat him! He smashed his fist at Ben's mouth, then lowered his head and butted, but Ben side-stepped. Thrashing like a windmill, John caught Ben off balance and pitched them both to the ground. They scuffled until Ben rolled on top.

"Injun lover." He thumped John's head against the dirt.

"No."

"Injun lover."

John squirmed and kicked and heaved. He tipped Ben over and, with all his strength, struggled to hold the bigger boy down.

A cold flood struck their heads and washed over them. The icy wave poured down until their teeth chattered.

"I'll fix you," came Ike's voice.

Slosh, landed another pailful, straight from Cold Spring Creek. The shivering boys scrambled up and stood, dripping and forming little puddles of mud in the dry, brown dust.

"Fighting by the mill! I'm ashamed. You hear it going. Do you want an explosion? You know better, both of you. And you, Ben, you're too big to fight John."

Ben said nothing, just wiped the blood from his mouth.

"I started it," John offered.

Ike was so angry that the fringe of his hunting shirt quivered. He looked John up and down. "You know better. I ought not to give you that tomahawk you were yelling about. As for you, Ben, you're jealous of the Indian boy. You're wrong. We need all the friends we can find—especially among the Indians. Now go fix that eye before it gets any blacker."

With a half-grin at John, Ben trailed away. John grinned back. He'd won the fight, almost. He could have kept Ben down if it hadn't been for that water. But he lost the grin when Ike turned on him.

"You're not to come near the mill when it's running—you or nobody else unless they have business with it. Now go to the edge of the clearing and stay there. I'll fetch the tomahawk."

In his turn, John trailed away. Still shivering, he sat on a stump until Ike hobbled back. If Ike got mad, he stayed mad. He was not like Ben. When Ben finished fighting, he had worked his mad off.

Ike handed John the tomahawk. "I don't know but what Ben's right. Your Indian may be a spy. I always said the only good Indian's a dead Indian, and I'm too old to change. But if you can make a friend, we need one. Now get," he ended.

John got. Reaching home, he hunkered down by the fence and looked about. His clothes still dripped water. He didn't want his mother to catch him. Wet clothes were bad; fighting was worse, and both together were sure to mean trouble.

Besides, he could never make it clear about the toma-hawk. Mother would say, "But, John, you didn't need it today. Tomorrow would do." In John's opinion, tomor-row never did do—and certainly not to learn throwing a tomahawk.

He peered about. No mother in sight. Good! There was Mary. Showing himself slightly, he beckoned her to come to him, but Mary disappeared. What was that stupid girl up to? There she came now, skipping as she swung a berry basket. She wasn't so stupid, after all, John admitted grudgingly.

"Ooh, but you're wet," said Mary. "What happened?"

"Nothing, where's Mother?" John was gruff.

"Nothing looks like fighting. Tell me who with or I won't help you."

"Ben Wills. He didn't want me to get the tomahawk, but I did." He showed it to Mary, who touched it gingerly.

"Him! I hope you beat him good, the big bully. Mother's out back. Hustle in quick or you'll catch it."

John made a run for the house and dived safely into the bedroom, where the Indian boy was resting. Then he glanced out the window. Mary must have decided to use the basket as long as she had it, for she disappeared behind the trees.

"Look, Ashara." John pulled the tomahawk from under his hunting shirt, wiped it dry against the blanket and handed it over. Ashara balanced it critically, letting the handle lie flat across his palm and the wide hatchet blade swing free.

"Good," he said. "You throw. I teach now." He swung his legs to the floor.

"Ashara!" exclaimed an angry voice. He jumped. "What do you think you're doing? Go right back to bed." Mistress Trimble stood in the doorway. She pushed a bowl of soup into the Indian's unwilling hands and said, "You stay in bed today. Tomorrow you can do whatever you want, but not today. Why don't you teach John some Onondaga?"

Leaving, she chuckled at the sight of the two boys standing forlornly in the middle of the room. John's shirt was wet, too. Obviously, he was expecting a scolding. Well, she had given him one pleasant surprise to make up for the other.

John looked ruefully at Ashara. Secretly, the Indian was happy. He hated to admit it, but now that he was standing up, his legs had a will of their own. They shook. He stiffened them long enough to crawl back into bed.

"Paleface mother wise, *royaneh*," Ashara agreed solemnly and sucked up the soup. "I teach Onondaga today; tomahawk tomorrow."

After a while, handing John the emptied dish, he said, "Call this *gatshi*."

"*Gatshi*," repeated John.

"*Tessehqua nene*."

"*Tessehqua nene?*" John looked blank.

"Dish go." The English words stumbled. "John make dish go."

"Oh!" Light dawned. "Put the dish away?"

"*Ganajori*—quick." Ashara nodded. When John returned, he asked, "*Otsajatshi?*" and answered for him, "John."

John tried it, "*Otsajatshi?*"

"Ashara."

The Indian boy pointed quickly to his eyes—*ogahra*, nose—*oniohsa*, mouth—*ixhagahroehnta*.

"Whew!" John whistled after his tongue had twisted around these names. As nearly as he could figure, the words seemed to groan their way up from somewhere in the stomach.

"Head—*anuwara*, hand—*eniage*."

Then Ashara pointed to the various parts of himself without speaking and made John name each.

"*Gawoenio*—that sounds well," the Indian admitted.

23

"How do you say gun?"

"*Gahsura.*"

"And bow and arrow?"

"*Aoena, gaheska* mean bow, arrow. *Hoh sarrichwagata. Anuwara nuwax.*" Ashara flopped down and pulled the homespun sheet clear over his head.

"What does all that mean?"

"Your questions no end. Head ache."

"Ache? I'll give you an ache," the white boy threatened and pounded Ashara in the ribs until Mary came running to know what the noise was.

"I brought you some strawberries. Tell me a story," she begged. "John, you haven't told me a story in a long time."

With a strawberry halfway to his mouth, Ashara stopped and looked stern. "Tell stories in winter. No tell when grass is green or snake come in bed, bee sting lip."

Mary looked with round eyes at the Indian. "They do? Why?"

"It is the custom. John, bring moccasins and a pebble. Play shell game instead."

Ashara picked up one of his own moccasins and, putting it in a row with the pair John had brought, he told Mary, "You watch, guess which moccasin I put pebble under."

Curls bobbing, Mary stood on tiptoe as his fingers flickered from moccasin to moccasin. When they stopped, she pointed. "That one." Ashara picked it up and showed the pebble lying below.

"Now let me try hiding it," she cried. Tongue caught between her teeth, she moved her hand quickly from one moccasin to another. Which to choose? Middle. Finally she looked up. "You both guess."

Ashara pointed to the right one and John to the left. When she lifted the middle moccasin triumphantly, they all laughed.

"I'll take you to Onondaga and win the tribe's fur," the Indian teased.

Mary clapped her hands. "Then we'll sail to France and buy gunpowder for the army."

"You need gunpowder?" Ashara's voice was eager.

"We need everything," John answered slowly. "Guns and powder and uniforms and food for the army. The British are coming from Canada to take away our land and our freedom, but we won't let them go without a fight."

"You need powder. Why you not make powder?" Ashara repeated.

"But we are!" Mary exclaimed. "We're trying, but we have to learn how. Only—oh, I forgot!" She clapped her hand to her mouth in consternation.

"Only the best comes from France," finished John bitterly. Mary had almost given away the secret; at least she had shown as clear as day that there was a secret. He turned and hurried out, afraid Ashara would ask questions he could neither answer nor toss aside. His heart was heavy; could Ashara be a spy, after all? His blood brother a spy?

Left alone, Ashara and Mary were quiet. Finally, Mary moved closer to the trundle bed. "Ashara?" she said timidly.

"Little sister?"

"I said something wrong. Will you forget I said it?"

Ashara pulled one of the golden curls showing beneath her bonnet. "Bright like sun," he murmured to himself. "Yes, I forget." He waved a hand. "Gone—like wind from air and snow from ground."

"Ashara, if John is your blood brother and I'm John's sister, then I'm your sister too, aren't I? I'm glad. I like you."

Ashara was startled. He had not thought of the bond as including anyone except John and himself, but Mary was right. When an Indian was adopted, he was adopted into the whole clan; the clan brothers were his brothers, the clan sisters his sisters.

"*Aquas toges, t'giatehnuntera*—that is surely true, my younger sister." He smiled. "No say powder. Now I sleep, get strong for trail tomorrow."

Mary leaned close. "*Niawo,*" she mimicked softly and slipped away.

"*Niawo*, Mah-ry, *niawo, Otquechtarocu,*" said Ashara. Tomorrow, he would teach John how to throw, how to smell out tracks and conceal his own. In a few weeks, his blood brother would be an Indian in the woods.

Where the afternoon sun slanted under the branches, John and Ashara lay with their shoulders propped against a big pine. This little hollow was John's favorite place, sheltered from the wind and surrounded by a tangle of bushes that hid it from all eyes but the sun's.

Reaching back to the sturdy trunk, Ashara said, "*Onehtah*—pine."

"*Onehtah,*" repeated John sleepily. He pushed back his heavy hair and, through half-shut eyes, admired the other's shaven head and scalp lock. Stretching, he sighed with content. He had practised with the tomahawk until his muscles ached, but the last throw had satisfied Ashara's critical eye. John had given the proper twist that sent the weapon flying to the mark.

Now Ashara rose. Jolted out of sleepiness, John sat up straight. "What are you doing?"

Ashara said nothing, but walked through the little hollow. A few steps ahead of him was the road and, a few more steps beyond, the secret entrance to the mill track. John's content fell away. Back into his head flew all his father's suspicions. Ashara would see the entrance; nothing escaped that sharp gaze.

Suddenly, the Indian knelt, watching eagerly up the trail. Without turning his head, he waved for John to come to him. The latter dropped flat and wormed his way across. He could see nothing.

Then his ear caught the light patter he had heard when he went to the mill. Runners again, one after the other, passing straight on as before, but headed the other way. The same pair, probably! They had seen Burgoyne and were coming back with a message.

Ashara pointed. "That way Fort George, then Falling Water, the big fort?" It was hardly a question, but John said, "Yes."

"Mohawk!" spat Ashara. "Join Yengeese."

"You're not Mohawk?" ventured John.

"Onondaga." Ashara returned to the pine tree. "Not Mohawk. Onondaga live west of Mohawks. There my father is chief of the people of the hills," he added proudly.

"Aren't the Mohawks and Onondaga friends? They both belong to the Iroquois Longhouse. But you don't sound friendly."

Ashara looked sad. "Iroquois Longhouse, that is Great League. Five tribes agree together. Now they quarrel and Longhouse break up. Some like Yengeese side; some like Wasto side."

"Wasto. Who do you mean, us?"

"You. Side against Yengeese. We call you Wastohehno —you come from Wasto." Ashara waved toward the east.

Wasto? John wondered. Not all the way east, across the ocean, because that would mean the Yengeese, from Britain. Where else could Ashara mean? Oh, Boston! Indians called Americans the Boston people.

"Longhouse break up," Ashara repeated, "Mohawk tribe like Yengeese side, Oneida like Wasto, Seneca like Yengeese, Onondaga and Cayuga say be neutral, wait."

Onondaga neutral, John thought. Then he's not against us. Aloud, he said, "Now what happens? Do they fight?"

"Great League will hold council; then tribes choose how they fight. They will not all choose the same, so no more Great League. Like leaves, Iroquois scatter. They blow before the wind. I not understand this war. Why sons fight father?"

"If you mean the British king, he's no true father," retorted John. "He doesn't want what's good for us. He just wants us to work for him. He sends soldiers here, so he can collect taxes that he has no right to. He sets what taxes we must pay and then he gives us no say about it. We may be sons, but we have some rights."

Ashara was thoughtful. "King should be like Indian chief. Chief lead way, not tell warriors must go here, if they want there. When chief do that, warriors not go. Where chief then?"

"That's it," John agreed. "The king should guide the colonies, but he forces them. So we have to stand up for ourselves."

Ashara picked up the tomahawk and struck idly at the tree. "Sometimes chief wrong. Sometimes he listen to bird that say warrior is wrong, when warrior not wrong. Then warrior must prove not wrong, prove not coward."

John thought, he means himself. He was sent out of the tribe or he ran away from it. That's why he only had the broken knife when I found him.

"Otquechtarocu, you fight war?"

"Yes. I want to join the army at Fort Ti," John explained. "Burgoyne is bringing the British down from Canada to capture it. Of course, he won't, but I want to help stop him."

"Then I help, too. Wyandot Indians fight on Yengeese side, and I fight Wyandot, old enemy. No one call Ashara coward again."

"Are they good fighters?" John shivered. What if they got past Fort Ti and attacked the powder mill.

"Wyandot snakes, but Wyandot brave." Ashara struck the tomahawk hard into the tree. "I go, find my father, tell him I fight with Otquechtarocu. I go now."

"Wait!" cried John, scrambling to his feet. "What about food?" Maybe if he got Ashara to the cabin, he could think of something to keep him. Father would be angry if the Indian got away.

"No need food. Only knife. Have brother's knife," Ashara said with a quick smile. "You practice tomahawk. by so many suns, I come." He held up all his fingers, then one hand again and was gone.

As if Ashara's leaving was a signal, the sky clouded over and rain began to fall. John looked up. Rain all spring, rain last week, more rain! Wearily, he pulled the tomahawk from the tree and started home alone. Ashara was no spy; he was coming back to fight.

Then a picture flashed into John's mind: Ashara kneeling by the road, waiting for the runners to pass. Was it all a ruse and was Ashara gone forever? Impossible! John scolded himself. What kind of a friend was he? Ashara had made him a blood brother by his own choice. His part was to trust the Indian and wait.

4

☆

FOR EVERY DAY that Ashara was gone, John marked a gash in the big pine. He was scraping the bark with the weak penknife he used now, when he heard hoofbeats and scrambled through the bushes.

Almost past, the express rider jerked on the reins. "You Captain Trimble's son? He sent me from Fort Ann to warn you. Ti fell."

"Fell? You said *fell?*" John caught at the horse's reins. "It can't! Not with three thousand men there."

"It has. The British hauled their big cannon to the top of Sugar Loaf Hill."

"But it's too steep. Cannon won't go up there. Everyone said—"

The soldier laughed. "Everyone said wrong. I saw the cannon myself."

"How did it happen?" John dropped the reins and clung to a tree for support. Ti—gone!

"You know Sugar Loaf? How the crag rises sheer out of the water about a mile south of the fort? Somehow, they made a road up the back, and there they were, looking down and laughing, ready to pot us like sitting ducks. We had to get out. Most of the men crossed the Lake to the Hampshire Grants, but two hundred of us, with Colonel Long, came up Champlain to Fort Ann. We brought the boats, filled with sick soldiers and guns and whatever we could save."

"You didn't even fight?" John could not believe this. To give up the fort without a blow!

"No chance," the express rider snapped. "The British held all the hills around the fort. As it was, we only made the Tail of the Lake a few hours before Burgoyne and his gunboats. He caught us there, unloading, so we had to burn everything and run for the Fort. The pine trees caught fire. I left the others there and came ahead."

"Why didn't you stay to fight?" asked John scornfully.

"For gosh sake, boy, I haven't time! The militia can fight, can't they? I have to deliver my messages. I'm not afraid of British nor Indians either. But the settlers are. They're coming down, scared stiff." The rider passed his hand around the top of his head, as if he were cutting a scalp.

"We're not scared," said John. "No Indians will drive us out."

Turning his horse, the rider left John stunned. Ti gone! That great shield at the head of the Lake fallen, and the enemy swarming across it, up the Lakes, past French Mountain to the attack! Losing the fort left the Hudson Valley wide open to the British and Indians. There were still Fort Ann and Fort George and Fort Edward, the three spread out on the routes Burgoyne might choose, but they were only palisades, really. The three together could not equal Ti. If Burgoyne could take Ti, he could take them, or he could even walk around them.

Running, John thought of the powder mill that they had hidden so carefully. If the British heard of it, they would hunt it out. John clenched his fists. He would never let them burn the mill. Ti's big guns were gone, but there was still the army. The mill must be saved to make powder for the army.

Those Indian runners he had seen and heard on the trail. Did they know that Ti would fall? Such a display of force was bound to swing the Iroquois over to the British side. The Iroquois were fierce. If they attacked, the frontier would go up in smoke. All the farms near the Lake would be burned.

When John panted out the story on reaching home, his mother whispered, "Ti gone, John, Ti gone?"

"But we aren't going? We'll stay?"

"Yes, your father will say so. Surely, he'll come soon, here or to the mill."

As the day dragged by, the rumors grew wilder; Burgoyne had passed the Tail of the Lake and burned Skenesborough. He was on Wood Creek; he was near Fort Ann. No, he would strike the other way, down Lake George to Fort George. His Indians were three miles away, two miles away. Listen, you could hear them whoop!

John caught up his gun. Wow! It was only Ben Wills, running as if all Burgoyne's Indians were after him.

"Ben," shouted John in disgust, "have you got to run as noisy at that? You'll bring the whole army on your trail. What's wrong at the mill?"

"Powder m-mill's all right," panted Ben. "British aren't to Fort George. Captain Trimble was at the mill. He says everyone's ordered to Fort Ann and help chop wood."

"Help chop wood? Leave the mill? It's a fine time!" John exploded.

"Nitwit! Across the road and up the road, so the branches jam. Schuyler's smart. Tangle the woods, break the bridges, throw stones in the creek. Make the swamps worse, see?"

John slapped at his gun. "Smart's right. Remember how much rain we had this spring, when we crabbed so? Now it's going to help us. And it rained all this week, too. The swamps by Fort Ann must be squashy."

"Bring your ax," Ben ordered. "Can you come early? We'll be there, Dick Jordan, too. Captain said there don't seem to be any British this way yet, but he don't know for sure. We don't have scouts, like the British have."

"If only Ashara were back," John wished. "He'd scout."

"Huh, that Injun, I still think he's a spy."

John aimed his gun, but Ben laughed and ducked. "I won't fight, mister, see you tomorrow," he called.

Start early, Ben had said. Dawn had barely streaked the sky when John set out for Fort Ann, gun across his elbow and ax swung head down in the other hand. He would skirt the south end of French Mountain, where the three tangled peaks stretched up, then strike east along the rough lumber tracks that led past the sawmills. Going by the other way, on the military road, south past the little blockhouse at the Half Way Brook to Fort Edward and then back north along the other fork of the road, would take too long.

In the half light, he groped between the big pines, early morning dampness clinging to his shoulders. Catching sight of a brown shirt ahead, he whistled soundlessly and ducked behind a tree. There was something familiar about the shirt, but even Tories looked familiar. Tories that were your own neighbors had joined the British and guided them straight to the American forts. Some were honest men, like the Skenes and the Jessups, who thought the British did right to punish the colonies. but some were only robbers, out for whatever they could get.

Brownshirt now, where did he fit in? John knew he had seen the man, with his loose stride and a leather patch across his shoulder. But who? As the rising sun struck the patch, John remembered. Dick Jordan, the old hunter! John whistled and the man spun in his tracks, gun leveled.

"John, you scared me! What's the idea, creeping up? I never thought you'd be that good a tracker. You could even fool me."

John was so pleased he could only grin in reply.

"Going to Fort Ann? I see your ax." The two swung into step.

"You chopping, Dick?"

The hunter nodded, "I know I always said, everybody to his own business. Let the British mind theirs; the colonies theirs. My business is hunting, not fighting, but now—well, I'm crowding sixty, but I can still outchop any man."

Secretly, John looked the hunter over. With his gun and buckskin suit, his powder horn slung by a strap over his shoulder, he seemed as well prepared to fight as chop.

John knew the horn had a map of the Lakes carved on it, and he asked to see this, because he could not figure why Burgoyne headed for Fort Ann.

"Me neither," said Dick, handing the horn over. "I carved this once. Many's the winter I spent up in the mountains and looked down on all this. Now see," he pointed, "here's the Lake sticking out from Canada like a long finger, that's Champlain. About halfway, another

34

finger branching off, pointing at your place, that's George. Ti sits exactly where George branches off, and they took Ti. Now, wouldn't you think they'd sail right up George to the head, where Fort George is?"

"Isn't the outlet bad, where George empties into Champlain?" asked John.

"All rapids, but the carry is only two miles. Then they'd sail up the Lake, sure it's against the current but what of it? Besides, they'd have that old road on the west side of Lake George, that the French cut when they fought us."

"I see." John studied the horn closely. "Then, once they reach Fort George, they take our road, past the mill track entrance, straight southeast to Fort Edward," he said.

"A good road that puts them right on the Hudson," Dick Jordan ended triumphantly. "But luckily they're not doing that. Instead, they sailed up Lake Champlain to the south end and got to Skenesborough. You ever been there?"

John shook his head. "I know Major Skene, but I was only there once. All I remember is the big stone house under the mountain, and an archway with PKS—1770 on it. I remember that because I wanted Father to have one with *his* initials and a date on it."

"The important thing is, there the lake runs sluggish, with narrow banks, not easy sailing like George. It's pole upstream all the way, to Wood Creek and then Fort Ann. From Ann to Fort Edward, they'll come by road; swampy. There's our chance, boy. It's only twenty miles to Edward, but we'll make Burgoyne sweat every mile. And when he does get to Edward, he's only where he could have been easier," Dick chuckled. "Nobody knows that's what—" He stopped abruptly, yanked his powder horn from John's surprised hand and pushed the boy into the underbrush.

35

So crushed against Dick that he could hardly breathe, John felt the hunter turn his head slowly. "Too late. They've seen us," Dick whispered. Across an open stretch, half bare of trees, three Indians flew toward them as if their moccasins had wings.

"No shots," warned Dick. "Strays from Burgoyne's army. May be more behind."

John gripped his ax and waited. He stared, fascinated, at painted faces with their blazing eyes almost hidden in the mask of color. Aiming at a black stripe down the forehead of one, he swung. The Indian crumpled, but the second, with an angry yell, threw himself at the boy.

Pinned to the ground, John could only make a half-stroke, but it sent the tomahawk raised above him spinning out of reach. He thrashed helplessly, his wind shut off by steady pressure. Through the buzz in his ears, he heard the scuffle as Dick fought the third Indian.

With a slow smile, the Indian reached for a knife, let it hang poised. Wishing it would drop and finish his futile struggle, John stared into the painted face. That Indian looks like Ashara, he thought, the same nose, the same mouth, but twisted with cruelty. Through warpaint, the eyes glittered as the blade slid down.

Then the knife was jerked loose, the hand torn away, and, with a ludicrous look of surprise, the Indian toppled sideways. Free, John struggled to his hands and knees, head hanging.

"That's the lot," said Dick Jordan.

John grabbed lungsful of air. "Th-thanks," he panted.

"Wouldn't want you to lose your scalp. Pretty good fighting for one man and a boy," said Dick in a satisfied tone while he surveyed the bodies of the three Indians, stretched out on the ground. "You want to scalp them?"

"No, no!" urged John. All he wanted was to leave there quick.

"Never held with it, much." Dick shrugged. "Too savage. John, look here. A blue-eyed Indian!"

Spitting on the buckskin rag that he wrapped about his gun, he wiped away the warpaint. John bent over the face with its white oval surrounded by the remnants of paint, its blue eyes staring sightlessly at the sky. He caught his breath and, snatching the rag from Dick, scrubbed harder.

"You know him?" Dick squatted nearby sympathetically while John worked.

"Don't you? It's Jim Park," moaned John and flung the buckskin across the smeared face, to shut out the sight of a past friend. "So this was the army he went to join! I thought he meant the Americans. No wonder Father looked queer when I told him."

"A friend of yours? You want I should fix him decent?" Dick asked, stirring the arms that lay wideflung on the pine needles. He could hardly bear to touch the body, even with his toe, but if John wanted him to—

John turned his back. Jim Park was dead, but Donald Macomber was alive, fighting for Burgoyne. Would they meet, too? "Leave him be. They're horrible! White men dressing like Indians and coming to kill their friends."

"Dirty trick," Dick muttered as he inspected the bodies. "Guiding Indians so they'll burn out old neighbors. Come along, John. Let's get to Fort Ann."

As the two walked away, they were followed by a derisive yell. One of the Indians leaped to his feet and spurted off in a zigzag race. Dick fired, but the Indian dodged at the flash and disappeared over the edge of the hill. John stood speechless.

"Played dead," grunted Dick. "Should have made sure of him. He was that last one."

"The one who looked like Ashara," John thought and started to say, "He reminded me of—"

"*Ssh,*" Dick interrupted him. "I hear drumming. Hurry!"

To keep up with Dick's loping trot, John ran.

The drumming grew louder every second. Finally, there was the fort, with its wooden stockade, the gate swung wide open on its leather hinges. What did they mean, leaving the gate open like that? John thought indignantly. He could see movement inside.

Out marched a straggling line of men, with a drummer boy at their head. "He's no bigger than I am," grumbled John, "and he belongs."

Captain Trimble, riding out on Black Bet, waved at the pair standing beside the road. John wondered what he meant, then realized with a start that he was waving them both into line. A slap from Dick rushed him forward and pushed him onto the ragged end.

"What's up?" he asked the homespun-shirted man next to him.

"You're out of step," the man grunted. John reversed, almost trotting to the sound of the drum. He asked again, "What's up?"

"We're after the British, dummy. They're right ahead— in the woods. Long's not the one to sit still when the British come."

John craned his neck. "That Long? Cheeky man sitting high on a bay horse?"

"Yep."

John admired the colonel. To walk out of a fort and try to stop the whole British army with this ragged line—

that was a fighter! Glancing over his shoulder he counted. There were five hundred at most and they were the poorest from Ti—the ones that rode down in boats, sick or lame or old. They were half out of line, each walking as he chose. Yet they meant defiance to the well-trained, well-equipped British ahead.

"We're attacking in front," the man told John, "while Colonel Van Rensselaer takes his men across the creek and hits them in back. You Trimble's son?"

"Yes," said John. Did it matter?

"It was your father that walked into the British camp this morning, just walked in calm as could be, pretending to be a deserter. He fooled them into thinking Fort Ann was so strong that they stopped by the hill over there. We've got to beat them. They beat us up at Skenesborough day before yesterday and made us burn the stores we brought from Ti. Hear that? We've met!"

Gunfire burst out ahead as the ragged band plunged through the woods. John's stomach felt queer, heavy, as if he had just eaten breakfast and didn't want to keep it down. Funny, because he had had breakfast before dawn and now it was ten o'clock. Then he felt Dick's hand press strong against his shoulder.

"Where are we?" John panted, sniffing. He could smell the gunpowder.

"By the ravine. It's narrow, between the creek and the hill. Sounds like the British are in there. Hurry," Dick whispered.

John heaved ahead. Suddenly fingers grabbed his ankle, pulled him down behind a log. "Whoa! You'd run straight into the British. See them by the hill," said Ben Wills, who had kept John from going blindly beyond the front line.

A stranger, kneeling at Ben's other side, pointed. "See 'em, those red patches in the trees? Got one," he yelled and fell backward, a wide hole torn in his chest. In a daze, John looked at the wound. He wanted to run, somewhere, anywhere, away from the whizzing death, but his legs would not move. Beside him, he could hear Ben sobbing aloud as he fired.

The British shot in heavy volleys, blindly, downhill, but in the American ranks, each man picked a target and aimed. Such accuracy was against old army habits. It disheartened the British and forced them backwards, while the smoke thickened.

In the ravine, the air hung heavy, with no breeze to carry off the powder fumes that wavered like a curtain between the armies. John rubbed the sting from his eyes. He'd get one for the stranger. A red coat flashed through the gray curtain, and he pulled the trigger. The British soldier slid down, twitched and lay still—dead. He had killed a man! He felt sick and, pressing his head against a rough tree trunk, tried to keep the forest steady. It seemed to reel around him.

"Baby!" he told himself furiously. "Are you a soldier or not? Your first battle, you act like a baby." But he could not raise his head from the comforting roughness of the tree's bark.

A hand shook him. "All right, Son?"

Captain Trimble was there, moving along the line of men, urging them ahead. "We'll beat them," he whispered. "Keep it up. Get them on the run. Van Rensselaer's men should strike any minute now."

John went ahead automatically, fire and load, fire and load. He didn't think about being sick now; he just fought. He would try for that rocky ledge, then dig in before the next push. The battle seemed to go on for hours, but the sun did not move and the shadows kept the same angle. It was not even noon yet. Would they fight all day?

The rocky ledge to which John struggled was the southern end of a high hill, where it squeezed close to Wood Creek, leaving only a narrow passsage between the two. Long meant to force the British away from the passage and push them uphill. Angrily, he ordered his men ahead, hammering at the British line.

John crouched by a tree with a tall man he did not know. Somehow he had lost Dick and Ben, as he climbed the hill. "Think we'll win?" he asked.

"Looks like it." The man spat in his hand to grease the bullets he held ready between his fingers. "Long's smart. He don't give up. Gol, what's keeping Van Rensselaer? Ought to be around their rear by now. . . . There he comes! Hear 'em holler!"

The man leaped to his feet and swung his musket. With a rattle of small arms fire that deafened John's ears, Van Rensselaer's men poured in on the rear. The British broke. Deserting their wounded and supplies, they fled uphill, where they packed into a tight ring, facing outward.

Swinging his line around, Long attacked, trying to smash the ring. John left the ledge that now seemed like an old friend and began to creep up the rocky slope—inch by inch, fire and load, cling for a foothold each time he moved.

Through the smoke and confusion, he caught a glimpse of his father, hurt, his shirt torn off and used for a bandage. John ran down the lines, heedless of bullets, heedless of a single high-pitched yell. Indians! They were coming to reinforce the British. The Americans hesitated. . . . Again that one yell.

John stopped. "Only one yell," he called out. "Maybe

it's a trick. Wait and see. You aren't scared by one yell?"
(He was right, though no one knew it until after the fighting. A British officer, bringing the Indians up to the battle, came on alone when they refused to fight. It was he who gave the Indian yell.)

The British seized their chance while the Americans hesitated and pushed forward. Captain Trimble vanished. John dived for the shelter of a log, but a weapon struck his head. His knees buckled and black curtains pressed around him.

5

☆

Y OU ALL RIGHT? That was my last bullet." Dick Jordan let water dribble across John's face.

The boy sat up, holding his head from flying apart. "Father," he mumbled, "got to find Father."

"He's all right." Dick pulled John to his feet. "Long's sent word to fall back, but not on account of the British. Ammunition's gone. Another hour, and we'd have had them, captured the whole force."

The shooting slackened off. Step by step and turning frequently to threaten the British with their empty guns, the American soldiers marched back to Fort Ann. Once there, Colonel Long looked the fort over critically. There were nothing but wooden sheds to serve as barracks, surrounded by wood palisades. He kicked a picket. It was old and rotten, indefensible if the British attacked—and the British were close on his heels. Squaring his shoulders, Colonel Long set fire to Fort Ann and led his men back to Fort Edward. All the way, he searched for a crest of land where he could fight if the enemy followed, but in the fourteen miles between forts, he found only flat ground, covered with giant pines and soggy from spring rains.

Dispirited, John and Dick joined the men that plodded through the heavy clay. None of them felt like talking. There was no sound but the squelch of shoes, sucked in and out of the mud, and the crackle of flames running up the tree trunks, leaping from top to top, where the burned fort had spread the fire that was started at Skenesborough.

Ben limped up, a bandage around his leg. "Beat 'em," he said cheerfully, "but where do we go? Backward."

"Fight hard like that, almost win—and then give up for lack of ammunition." John was grim as he dragged his tired feet out of the sticky clay. This proved how much they needed the powder mill. If only they could keep it going, keep it a secret from the British. Burgoyne's prowling Indians must be near. He prayed they would not find it.

If his father could—Where was his father? John looked up and down the column. Nowhere could he see Captain Trimble nor Black Bet. The tall horse would show over a man's head. He found Colonel Long's bay and some other officer on a chestnut mare, but not Black Bet.

A cloud of dust moved up the road and dissolved into Captain Trimble, who spoke hastily to Colonel Long, then wheeled Bet around. John ran out of line.

"Father," he called. Captain Trimble pulled up, embarrassed to be stopped from the ranks, even by his own son.

"What is it, John?" he asked impatiently, holding Bet in check by one hand.

"I—just want to know if you're all right. I saw you get hurt."

"I'm fine. Bones in my hand nicked, that's all."

"It was such a funny battle. Everyone in a different fight of his own, sort of hand to hand. I didn't think fighting a battle was like that."

"Tell you a secret." The captain leaned down. "All battles are like that. A hundred little fights in one. The side that wins the most little fights wins the big one."

"Well, we won that big one," said John with satisfaction. "Did you get the guard for the powder mill?"

"I got a guard of one." The captain chuckled. "Me," he explained at John's puzzled face. "The general said no guard, but for me to stay home until my hand is well. At least I can help at the mill, while you're at Fort Edward, chopping. Burgoyne chose the worst route, and we can stop him." Captain Trimble slapped Bet's rump to start her galloping.

But few soldiers had Captain Trimble's faith, and John, by the time he arrived at Fort Edward, was sunk in gloom with the others. Even the thought of his father being home did not cheer him. There was no hope of a reinforcement for the powder mill. There was a rumor of burning Fort George, which would leave the road open to the enemy.

Worst of all, news came that the British had caught St. Clair's army, beaten it and made it retreat for miles before it could double back to Fort Edward. Now here they were, cooped up in a fort, supposed to be strong, though any fool could see that British cannon balls, directed from

44

the hills around it, would sweep across the inside. Cooped up, with no shelter but brush huts that leaked rain like a sieve, powder down to five rounds a man, no food. Nothing had been saved from Ti, all supplies lost with the fort that was their shield.

John paced the crumbling walls. "Humph," said Dick. "Burgoyne's not here yet. You did well at the battle, and now you want to quit because it's time to work? Get busy. Where's that ax you carried before?"

Meanwhile, the British, left on the hilltop near Fort Ann, also retreated. Though more soldiers had been sent to rescue them, they were too shaken to hold their ground. Moving back to Skenesborough, where the Lake was close, they left Sergeant Lamb to care for the wounded, who lay in a small hut near the battlefield. Disconsolate, the men huddled in the rain that began to pelt down, while the Sergeant tried to dress wounds without any medicine. Day after day, they waited, fearing a summons to surrender that never came. During the nights, from their hut, they heard the thud of falling trees, the thump of rolling stones, sometimes even the shouts of men.

The savagely rough ground was choked with timber, felled by American woodsmen, who laid the trunks crisscross and jammed the branches so tight that the British must spend weeks in chopping a passage through. The creeks were dammed with rocks until water backed through swamps and ravines. Burgoyne would pay for every step his men walked, every foot of road his guns rolled. The British Army, that had traveled so gaily from Ti, was bogged down.

Along Wood Creek, the swamp was full of blueberries and mosquitoes, especially mosquitoes. John, working with

Ben Wills and Dick Jordan, shifted his crowbar to one hand and slapped. Men everywhere, plastered with the stingers, slapped steadily. Dick slapped, Ben slapped, John slapped. Then he seized a handful of blueberries and crammed them into his mouth. Ugh, he spit them out, not so ripe as they looked! He slapped again, reached for the crowbar and pried viciously. Another rock tumbled into Wood Creek.

"Who thought we'd be back in this swamp so soon when we left Fort Ann?" he called to Ben. "Tough on the soldiers that have to clear this out. Does Burgoyne think he's in London, that he can bring guns and wagons?"

"I hear they're building one bridge two miles long," said Dick. "Ti-i-i-mber," he yelled, and the boys jumped back. They watched the tree crash down, to lie with its top spread across the bed of the creek, its branches upstream.

"Nice tangle that makes to chop through." Dick nodded approvingly. Mopping his head, he came to stand with the boys. "Ben, look out behind!"

With all his strength, he smashed his ax to the ground, just beyond Ben. "Copperhead." He pointed. "Finish him."

John spun around. Cut almost in two, a chunky-headed copper and chestnut snake thrashed in the mud. After flailing at it with his crowbar, John flung the body into the bushes.

"Rather get my scalp lifted than bit by poisonous critters," said Dick. "You boys come out of that water and chop with me. It's safer. Plenty of rocks in this stretch, anyways. Drop some trees in and we'll be done."

Taking position, one on each side of a big pine, Ben and John swung their strokes in rhythm. "Hope those soldiers guarding us ain't dreaming," panted Ben. "We're making enough noise to bring a swarm of Indians."

"Guess they're after settlers to burn out." John's answer was distracted. This pine had reminded him of Ashara and the pine on which he had started to count the days before the Indian's return. His blood brother must come soon now. He had held up fifteen fingers, and seven were used up on the morning John met the express rider.

"I hope I'm home by the time he comes," John thought. "If Ben only liked Ashara, we could talk about him."

"Ben," John tried it.

"Well?" Ben stopped whistling.

"You don't still think Ashara's a spy?"

"You bet I do." Ben made each ax stroke cut viciously. "Don't his leaving here prove it? He goes one week and the next week we're fighting."

"Proves nothing." John's ax cuts were landing as hard as Ben's. "Suppose he came back and fought on our side."

"He won't. Injuns are all the same." Ben began to whistle again, hard enough to drown out any answer the boy could make. John gave up the argument and chopped in silence.

As long as it wasn't true, he didn't care what Ben thought. Ashara would come; he knew that. His friend might even come now, while John was still chopping in the drowned lands on Wood Creek.

When the working party returned wearily to Fort Edward, the sentries urged them along. "Getting dark. You want to lose scalps?"

"Humph," said Dick, shifting his ax from one sore spot to another, "what else we got you for? They'll take your pretty scalps instead. Nothing to do all day but lean on a

47

you are like him. You and Ashara would like to join the army together, I imagine?"

"Oh, yes," John's words tumbled out eagerly. "I'm old enough. I'm older than the drummer at Fort Ann."

"You did well in that battle. I took pains to find out." General Schuyler was amused at John's startled face. "But until you are sixteen, you can enlist only with your father's permission."

The general twirled his quill pen. He could hear John's gulp and gave him time to swallow his disappointment. "The mill is an important post, John, because we need the powder. Sooner or later, Burgoyne must use the Lake George route. Then his wagons will move down the road, directly across the entrance to the mill track. Then, too, he may order roadmakers to widen the road. That's why I am sending you home tomorrow, before the chopping is finished. You're tired of it?"

John shook his head, but the general laughed. "Be honest. I know you're tired of mosquitoes. Take Ben Wills along because he is needed at the mill. As for you, John, ask your father to lend you his horse—"

"Black Bet?" John interrupted eagerly.

"Yes, if she is the one you like to ride. See how poor my army is, all the horses are moving supplies south, and I must borrow yours."

"Oh, Father will lend her gladly," promised John, wondering what was on General Schuyler's mind that made him stab at the table with his pen.

Evidently reaching a decision, the general tossed the quill aside and picked up his pipe. Tamping down tobacco with quick fingers, he lowered his clear, sharp voice. "I tell you in confidence, John, what your father already knows. Burgoyne is right about the Tories. This district, especially around Albany, is full of them. Many others, once my bravest soldiers, are discouraged and deserting. No militia regiment would come here with me. I came alone, and as to the few men I found here already, how long before they go?"

"The Trimbles won't go. You can depend on us." And forgetting the General's lame leg, John thumped the floor with his ax until the boards shook.

With an effort, Schuyler kept his hand from the stool. Instead, he took a deep pull on his pipe. "I do depend on you. So take Black Bet and ride to the sawmills—Wing's, Cheshire's, Hufnagle's, all of them. See that the ironwork is hauled away. Iron is scarce; we can't spare any to the British. If you find anything left, so much as a scrap, report to me. Look out for Tories, and when Ashara comes, bring him here. You understand?"

"I ride to the mills and then report to you. Yes, sir, I'll start right in." John was so excited he swung the ax from hand to hand as he ran to share his news with Ben.

"No more chopping. Tomorrow we go home. Back to the mill."

Ben jumped to clear the ax. "Whoa there, you needn't chop off my leg! I want to go, too."

John laughed and swung again. Best of all—he hugged his secret to himself—he was going back to wait for Ashara. If Ben knew that, wouldn't he be mad?

6

☆

ALFWAY UP THE HILL, John propped himself against the stony cleft in his old friend, Blind Rock, and counted the score. He had been to Jones's, the Tory Hufnagle's, Wing's, Cheshire's, even to the two little sawmills on Rocky Brook, where it flashed along the ravine by French Mountain. Was he finished? He had stopped between Fort Edward and Fort George, so he could backtrack either way.

Counting, he tapped against the rock with the one piece of iron he had found, a ring-dog from Hufnagle's. Yes, he was done. All the ironwork had been stripped away, sawblades, chains, everything. Only logs lay deserted in the clearings, where the ox teams had dragged them.

Schuyler's men had worked well. They were Continental soldiers, not like the militia that had arrived at last, some at Fort George and some at Fort Edward. They were miserable looking men, shivering in the brush huts that leaked rain, scared to leave these shaky shelters, scared of Indians, scared of their own shadows. They had no sooner reached the forts than they ran away home, leaving Schuyler at Fort Edward with only his seven hundred Continentals to defeat eight thousand British. How could seven hundred stop eight thousand?

John sighed, dog-tired. He ought to go on, but finally decided he would stay here and rest until he heard the evening gun from Fort George. It was good to hear the deep note ring across the hills. It echoed among the peaks of French Mountain with a solemn reassurance. Waiting, he edged around Blind Rock and gazed up at French Mountain. They were old friends, both of them, landmarks of courage. Blind Rock stood up from the swampy country around it with a stubborn strength, and French Mountain soared as if it had heart to pierce the sky.

A pebble clattered. Dropping the ring-dog, John stared. Something shone between his feet, white in the sun. It was a perfect arrowhead, the point aimed at the road. A warning? Burgoyne's army was still in the rough ground between Fort Ann and Fort Edward, working to bridge the swamps, but his Indians ranged far ahead.

John froze, his eyes searching the woods. By the foot of a pine tree, an Indian stood. John squinted to make out the figure, then whooped with joy.

"Ashara, you returned! Is the arrow yours?" He dropped to the pine needles beside the Indian.

"Arrowhead for my brother," Ashara answered in Onondaga, as he always did now with John. "Otquechtarocu has no *orenda*, no medicine bag from the gods, and that is well, for he has not dreamed. A warrior must fast and dream, to be given *orenda* from the gods. But Otquechtarocu needs a talisman against danger, so while I am there, I chip arrowhead of white flint from the Sacred Place."

Pulling a strip of rawhide from his pouch, Ashara twisted it on the notched stem and hung the arrowhead around John's neck, saying, "Now my brother is safe. This will protect him."

"*Niawo.*" John fingered the flint and the strip of rawhide that Ashara had painted red. "My brother is kind. My brother is a warrior. Therefore he dreamed?"

With a quick intake of breath, Ashara put his hand to his pouch. "An outcast carries no medicine in his bag. But I dreamed, yes. I dreamed of the *hinon*—the little feathered bodies. They are my helpers, but without my medicine bag, I do not know if they can help me. Let us speak no more of dreams, for They Who Listen will not be pleased. I brought news. Have you heard?"

"Nothing new," John answered.

"To the north, on the Narrow Lake, there are Yengeese soldiers. A friend of my father's told me. He did not say where they are going."

"By the Narrow Lake? Why there? That is off the straight route, and someone should find out—Ashara, listen. General Schuyler wants us to scout for him, but we can't go now. He went to Albany and he's not back yet. Why don't we scout by the Lake?"

"Only two? *Aquas 'nt'wodejenoni*—we must be cautious. But we know the woods and they do not, the clumsy simpletons. I think they make a road."

"A road! They must be fixing the old one, on the west side of Lake George. We've got to find out, on account of—" John gulped, then continued, "On account of something I must not tell you. How soon can we start?"

"Now, why wait? We'll go upstream to the portage, then by river to the Narrow Lake. I have parched corn to eat. Come."

When the pair reached the water, Ashara motioned John into a canoe. "We'll stop at the portage. Uphill is a cave that few know of, except my cousin. There we can— *Hist, toh!*"

Across the water floated a gay whistle that evidently came from a white man in buckskin.

"He has not noticed us," said Ashara. "Hold your paddle edgewise, so as not to splash water. We'll carry the canoe." With a driving stroke, they shot under the hanging bushes, picked up their guns and disappeared behind the forest screen.

"Here—a cache for the canoe!" Urgently, they pushed the craft into a hollow log and Ashara rearranged the bushes. As he waited, John idly pulled at a leaf, creased it and was about to let go when he realized that even so small a sign could betray them. Rolling it into a ball, he tucked it into the log's mouth.

Ashara pointed at two squirrels playing tag on a nearby tree. John motioned to his gun and shook his head.

"*Ohne,*" agreed the Indian. "I try knives." Holding out his hand for John's pen knife, he balanced a knife on each hand. One after the other, they flashed, the heavier toppling both squirrels to the ground. Gathering up his game and the two knives, Ashara climbed to where three clumps of bushes formed a triangle. In the middle lay a heap of fallen rock.

"This will mark the place," he said. "The top stone is like a face, and you follow where he looks. The cave is here."

Ashara vanished. John squeezed between two stones and followed him. "This is fine," he whispered when the faint light of their fire showed the cave around them. Only in the middle was the roof high enough to let them stand upright, but the walls felt strong and dry.

"Now that you know the place, it is your cave, too," said the Indian boy.

When the aroma of cooked squirrel meat seeped through

the cave, they grinned at each other and sat forward in anticipation. Suddenly, John felt Ashara's hand on his leg. He rolled his eyes to the left. Without moving a muscle, the Indian sat, ears fixed, nostrils distended. John's scalp prickled.

Ashara turned, his lips against John's ear. "I hear nothing. It is too quiet. You stay." Picking up the gun, the Onondaga crawled cautiously out. John lay in the doorway and listened.

Above the cave, crouching with his ear to a crack, was a sullen-faced Indian with a bedraggled feather drooping from his scalp lock. Restlessly, he fingered his tomahawk and then laid it aside. He stiffened. Behind him, moccasin slid against rock. Ashara had spotted him and was creeping up in back. The Indian raised his gun, fired and crashed down the hillside.

Ashara sent a bullet flying after him. John dashed out of the cave, and with thumping hearts, the two boys followed the crack and splinter of undergrowth.

"H-he may ambush us ahead," panted John as he struggled to catch up.

Ashara paused. "Or lead us to his friends. *Jahgatnte shegehha?*" he asked.

"*Jachte khegehha!*" John shook his head.

"If you had seen him, you would know him another time. That was my cousin."

"Your cousin! Aren't you friends? You're hurt."

"Just a scratch. He's a poor shot. He would rather use his tongue." Ashara's eyes flashed. "We were friends until he turned against me. He seeks mischief—*garrihwahetke honohtonnie.* I heard that he was seen lately with the Yengeese."

Back at the cave, Ashara placed his hand where his cousin had knelt. "He was not here long."

"But he could follow us all day," John objected.

Ashara touched his friend on the shoulder. "Too lazy. A better scout would have made no noise in those bushes."

The squirrels were nearly burned, but to John, alone in the cave with Ashara, the firelight red on the walls, they tasted delicious.

After swallowing the last scrap, he leaned forward to ask, "What do we do at the Narrow Lake?"

"It all depends," Ashara replied, "on how many Indians this party has. Sleep now. I will keep watch."

John rolled close to the dying fire and curled into a ball. As he studied his friend's face in the flickering light, he wondered. Ashara had said nothing about his trip. Sworn brothers though they were, John would never know the Indian's depths. But Ashara, he thought with a wry grin, probably knew his. He remembered what had been said of old Judge Hutchinson. Ashara was like that: a deep well you could drink from but never reach the source. Other words came to John's mind, "We were friends until he turned against me."

Somehow the latter words recalled the Indian fight near Fort Ann. Was that cruel-faced Indian Ashara's cousin? By some strange chance, had John already met him? If so, they would meet again and not, John vowed, for the cousin's good.

Next morning, the air shone clean after a light rainstorm. By the canoe, John bent to pick up a feather.

"*Toh'n gecto*—give it to me." Ashara held out his hand. "My cousin's. See the string on the quill? He went this way and is before us. Trouble-maker." Ashara scornfully tossed the feather aside and motioned to John to launch the canoe.

Where the river widened into a lake, he headed for shore. "We will scout, I west, you east, and meet soon by that oak."

On reaching the oak, some time later, John found Ashara already there, flattened against the trunk. "A Seneca passed," the Indian explained, "but he was watching the trail ahead. He never saw me."

"If the Senecas are this far from their ground, the British must be with them. Ashara, what can they be after? Scalps?"

"Not the British. They want something else." As John pulled desperately at his hair, thinking hard, Ashara waited. How much would his brother be willing to tell him? Finally he spoke, "Otquechtarocu, they could go by this lake to Fort George, but have you thought? They may be after your home."

"Home!" John thought of his family, left without soldiers to protect them, except for his father, who was wounded. Then he threw his scruples to the wind. How could he hide the secret from Ashara any longer? "Listen, they're after the powder mill. It's hidden in the woods, where we thought they would not come."

"*Gawoenio*," Ashara nodded, and silently the two launched their canoe and paddled on.

Where a spit of land jutted into the lake, they heard voices calling, "This way. There's a fine spring here." There was an exclamation as a dash of cold water evidently flew in someone's face. "And here's better for you, Bill," came the quick challenge.

John crept over to Ashara. "Can you slip away and let them find me?" he whispered. "I'll tell them I'm lost."

"*Ohne,*" muttered the Indian as he dropped over the side of the canoe, swam ashore and glided into a crevice between some scattered logs. John slid after him, then, reaching out, gave the canoe a slight push and let it drift. He quietly followed it along the shore.

"Hey, there's a canoe! Indians hidden in it!"

"You and your Indians! Pull it in—got it."

John, peering through the bushes, saw five or six British soldiers with water buckets. They stood clustered around his canoe. John deliberately snapped a twig underfoot. As the men whirled about, he pretended to hesitate, then ran. Picking out a convenient log, he tripped over it.

"Get up!" A bluff looking sergeant loomed above him.

John flung a hand over his head. "I—I ain't done noth-in.' "

"What are you here for? No one lives here."

"I was huntin' in the woods far up, when I got lost and followed the lake," he twisted his shirt in his fingers and sniffled, "to see if it would take me to some settlement. I'm awful hungry."

"You've got a gun," said one of the soldiers, eyeing him sharply. "I never heard of any colony boy getting lost in the woods."

"But only one bullet, and I kept that for a bear. I wanted a bear for my Aunt Jane in New York, but not now. Please, sir, tell me how to go home."

The sergeant in charge of the party laughed. "Cheer up. You're safe. We're going to the captain."

As they tramped along, John thought of Ashara, left hiding in the crevice, and cast a wary glance about for some way to signal him.

"None of that! March along."

59

Pretty soon, ahead of them appeared a neat camp, the underbrush cut away, the tents pitched in regular files. John snorted scornfully. Imagine soldiers lugging tents when the whole forest was there to cut rough shelters from!

"Stay here." The sergeant ordered a couple of soldiers to keep an eye on John and started toward the biggest tent. Presently he returned. "You'll have to wait. The captain's busy. Don't leave camp or it will be the worse for you!"

All afternoon, as John hung around, he felt that someone watched him. Once he thought he saw an Indian duck behind a tree, and he wondered if it could be Ashara's cousin. He bit his lip. He didn't like being spied on this way. He wanted a chance to hide by the captain's tent without being observed.

When dusk crept across the clearing, a candle shone from the tent. Now was his chance. Most of the soldiers were gathered around the campfires, eager for the food that was being prepared for them. For quite a while, John lay motionless on a huge log. Finally, he rolled quietly to the far side and crawled along in back of it.

Once behind the tents, he made for the gleam of candle-light coming from the captain's quarters and pressed close against the canvas to listen. He heard the captain's voice.

"Rough trail from there. . . . Get that mosquito, O'Hara . . . ten men. . . . Congreve, at Fort George cut off. . . . That boy, can't let him go. . . . What's the noise? Oh, Indians back!"

John, frantically trying to piece the words together to make sense, suddenly realized that he had been hearing shouts for some time. He ducked away from the captain's tent and ran to where many of the soldiers were crowded together.

The Indian scouts had returned. They were silhouetted against the glare of the fires. John strained his eyes to make out their tribe. One crossed close to the light. That one, so young, could it be—?

John gasped and wormed his way into the crowd. Yes, it was Ashara himself, surrounded by his enemies! He looked toward John with idle curiosity, looked away. The white boy tried to keep his face expressionless, although his heart was thumping.

"Boy, you said you were lost." The captain had come from his tent and now stood behind John.

"Yes, sir, I was—I am."

"You weren't lost this way on purpose? Odd we pick up so many stragglers. You know this one?"

John and Ashara were swung face to face. "No, sir," answered John. "I don't think so. I don't know Indians very well." At least, that much is true, he thought.

"The sergeant says you have an aunt in New York." The captain frowned and struck one fist on the other palm.

"The Widow Lester. She boards some of the British officers. Perhaps you know her, sir?" John neglected to add that, though his aunt was a Tory, he himself was not.

"No," the Captain said, "but the place is full of Loyalists, all whining about how badly the Rebels treated them and how much property they used to own. Find a place to sleep, and I'll settle your case tomorrow." He strode away, his spurs jingling smartly.

John crouched down to watch Ashara from the darkest spot he could find. If only they would not fasten him wrist to wrist with one of the Indians! He soon found that they were binding his legs together and leaving him where he was.

After enduring a seemingly endless wait until the camp

61

had quieted down, John groped for his penknife and, holding it ready, began to crawl the long way to his fellow-prisoner. A few inches and listen, a few inches more and listen. John wished it were Ashara tracking him. How smoothly the young Indian would have crossed the ground. Only a little more to go. Now by stretching, he could reach his friend's feet. He cut at the bindings. They were too tough—they weren't going to give! But they *had* to give. John sawed violently. There, one strand parted, then another, then the last. John crawled up to Ashara's hands and cut again.

"John." It was only a breath. "*Tagehqua*—help me up. You go first. I'll meet you at the big sycamore on the edge of camp."

"Take my knife. You may need it. They don't watch me so closely."

For a while, John crawled. When he was almost to the sycamore, he stood up and looked back for Ashara. Suddenly he felt the grip of a hand and heard a muttered, "What you do here?"

Lunging, he grabbed for the strange Indian's knife. Hands locked, the two strained to free the weapon. Another figure loomed overhead, and the stranger went limp.

"My cousin, but only stunned." Ashara's voice was grim. "Otquechtarocu, are you hurt?"

"No. Look for his knife."

"I have it. The one you gave me. He stole it when they took me. Did you learn anything?"

"They're going for the mill."

"Push on, then, straight to the lake and never mind our trail. They will search there, anyway."

John was soon panting as he ran, but Ashara raced easily over the ground. Finally, they felt gravel under their moccasins. "*Sajatagunte*," said the Indian. Obediently, John stood still. The two listened intently but heard no sounds of pursuit. They tumbled into the canoe and drove eastward with steady strokes.

"Ashara, how did they catch you?"

"I watched the scouts come along shore. When they got near camp, I shifted around it and ran straight into another party—mostly Senecas, with a few Onondagas. I tried to convince them I was friendly, but my cousin let them know about me."

It was almost dawn. Leaving the canoe, they shoved it well out into the lake and plunged under the forest cover, just as the early bird chorus filled the air.

Ashara whispered, "We must cover our trail but lose no time, either."

John stepped carefully where Ashara pointed and, finding bare rock, they toiled up the ragged face of a cliff.

"We're getting up but not on. Maybe they won't bother to trail us," John grumbled.

"No chance," retorted Ashara. "Not with my cousin to warn them." He lay along the ledge and looked back. "There, four of them, almost across the lake. Hurry!"

Again they scrambled up the rocks. Ashara had just found a faintly marked trail along the crest when they heard a soft whistle and a low call, "John!" Standing at the base of a boulder, blending with it in color, was a man dressed in buckskin. It was Dick Jordan.

"What are you doing here?" all three asked simultaneously.

John was the first to answer. "We ran into some Indians, and they're chasing us." He spoke briefly, for he was puzzled. Now he remembered that it was Dick they had seen before, paddling the other way.

The hunter seemed to read John's mind. "I've been scouting for your father. He fears the British will learn of the mill."

"They have," John broke in. "But at Fort Ann you said you had no use for politics."

Dick winked. "A useful pose. Are Indians after you?"

"Look!" Ashara pointed. Far below were the trackers. Every few minutes, they consulted over the trail. John shivered. Their bare brown bodies almost fading into the brown of the rocks, the Indians hunted relentlessly.

"Suppose they don't find us," Dick suggested. "No use to give ourselves away. But if they do, I can pick them off easily while you warn the mill." He settled down to watch, while the other two sped on.

"I hope Father's home," John thought. "If he isn't, I'll have to tell Ike and no one could make him budge from that mill, even to save his scalp."

At long last, the two boys reached their goal, and John pulled the latch-string. As the door swung open, to his vast relief, he saw his father and poured out the story.

"Someone must warn the fort," said Captain Trimble. "Will you saddle Black Bet and go?"

"Oh, yes. Can Ashara ride Star?"

At the captain's nod of consent, the boys ran for the horses.

7

☆

WITH NO TIME to spare, the two horses pounded down the trail. At the military road, Ashara pulled up Star and asked, "Which way? Edward? George?"

John hesitated, then answered thoughtfully, "Edward's farther. We're a long way from the blockhouse at Half Way Brook and twice that to the Fort. The general may be at Edward. He will believe us, if he's there. But George is nearer. I don't like Major Yates, but that doesn't matter. We ought to warn him. Come on."

He slapped Black Bet and raced toward Fort George, with Ashara following. The road ran through unbroken woods. It was dark under the pines. Finally, they burst out into the light, on the heights that fronted the Lake.

Shading his eyes, which were blinded by the glare after the forest darkness, John swept a quick glance along the water. It lifted and splashed lazily, the waves tipped with gold by the sun. No black dots moved across the surface. He sighed in relief. The British were not yet using this open route from Fort Ti.

Tugging at his arm, Ashara pointed. Below them, near the shore, still a mile ahead, lay Fort George, its unfinished star-shape cut straight across by a rough wall, left without ditch or picket to protect it. The fort was an old sight to John, but today he could hardly see it, nor the sawmill on the edge of the marsh, nor the long wooden sheds built for a hospital. All were hidden behind a cloud of dust. The fort looked anything but peaceful, why, the fort looked—

"Evacuating?"

"*Ohne*," confirmed Ashara. He had wondered what had scored the deep ruts he had seen in the military road. Now he would learn.

"Going?" John was bewildered. "Evacuating without a word to let us know! How can they?"

Ashara did not hear. He had never seen anything like this in all his life, and he stared, absorbed, at the ox team. More dust rose as the great beasts, wooden yokes creaking, tails swishing, maneuvered their load through the gate. Another team, waiting to enter, jingled the long chains that linked pair to pair. "Gee, haw!" the drivers' voices bawled out. "Easy there, Beauty. Gee, haw! Hup Mike, pull."

"Gee, haw!" Ashara practiced the new English words softly. What were the teams pulling? He rose as high on his horse as he could. There, the team was out of the gate at last. Cannon! Taken apart and tied on a rude sled, the fort's cannon were being hauled away.

"There's Major Yates!" John guided Bet down the hill and through the confusion of sweating teams, shouting drivers and hurrying soldiers.

"Sir, I have an urgent private message."

"From General Schuyler? He sends strange messengers." The major's eyes flicked hastily over the boys and returned to watch the ox teams pulling cannon, food and powder out of the fort.

"Not exactly, but this Indian, Ashara, and I are scouts for General Schuyler."